ALONE AT HOME

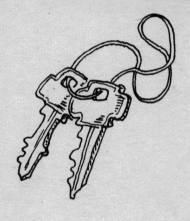

ALONE
AT HOME

By Barbara Shook Hazen
Illustrated by Irene Trivas

Troll Associates

To Mary Lou and Bernie,
whose special recipe for friendship keeps me
from being alone at home in Otis

Atheneum
Macmillan Publishing Company
866 Third Avenue
New York, NY 10022

Maxwell Macmillan Canada, Inc.
1200 Eglinton Avenue East
Suite 200
Don Mills, Ontario M3C 3N1

Macmillan Publishing Company is part of the Maxwell
Communication Group of Companies.

First edition
Printed in the United States of America
10 9 8 7 6 5 4 3 2 1
The text of this book is set in 12/16 Aster
Library of Congress Cataloging-in-Publication Data

Hazen, Barbara Shook.
Alone at home/by Barbara Shook Hazen: Illustrated by Irene Trivas.
p.   cm.
Summary: Amy experiences some scary moments when she finally
gets the chance to babysit herself.
ISBN 0–689–31691–7
[1. Self-reliance—Fiction.   2. Growth—Fiction.   3. Fear—
Fiction.]   I. Trivas, Irene, ill.   II. Title.
PZ7.H314975A1   1992   [E]—dc20   91–15878

Book design by Tania Garcia

ONE

AMY was proud of all the things she could do all by herself now that she was bigger.

She could braid her own hair, and most of the time it turned out okay. She could roller-skate and she could read better. She could go to the corner Mini Mart alone.

But there were other things she still wanted to do. One of them was to baby-sit herself.

Amy liked to think of all the fun things she could do if Mrs. Muldoon wasn't around. She could see herself munching Choco-bars and watching TV cartoons. She could see herself lying on the floor with her feet on the sofa instead of the way Mrs. Muldoon made her sit.

Amy kept asking, "When will I be big enough to baby-sit myself?"

Her parents kept saying, "Soon."

"When is soon?" Amy asked her mother one day when her mother was measuring her.

Her mother had a ruler in her hand and a pencil in her mouth. She said, "Hmmmmm."

Then she said, "You're a whole inch taller. That's a lot."

Amy was pleased. Taller was almost as good as bigger.

"Then can I baby-sit myself?" she asked.

"Ask your father," her mother said as she marked the wall. "And get ready for school. I've got a ton of work to do."

"I am ready," Amy said as she skipped down the hall. "Ask your father" was better than "Soon."

Her father was in the bathroom shaving. Amy could hear the hum of the electric shaver.

She knocked on the door.

"Come in," he said.

Amy did. She waved to her father in the mirror. She remembered when she was too small to see into the mirror.

She sat down on the edge of the tub and said, "Mom said to ask you if I'm big enough to baby-sit myself."

"Oh, she did, did she?" Amy's father gave Amy a funny look.

"Then can I?" Amy asked. "Chris does."

"Chris isn't you."

"And Lars does."

"Lars isn't you either. You are what counts to us."

"We could save tons of money," Amy leaned forward and said. "Enough to go to McDonald's. That way you and Mom wouldn't have to cook."

"Now, that's a thought," Amy's father said as he splashed his face with smelly stuff.

"So can I?" Amy asked as he splashed some on her too.

"When you're big enough to pick up your school bag so I don't trip over it," her father said. "And when you're big enough to remember Hermie's water. Without being reminded."

Amy gulped, got up, and raced into her room. Hermie, her hamster, was in his cage washing his leg. His water tube was empty. Completely empty.

"Uh-oh," Amy sighed. It seemed that no matter what she did, it was never enough.

TWO

IN the kitchen, Amy got the Cocoa Critters down from the kitchen shelf. Last year she had had to stand on tiptoe to reach the cereal shelf. This year she didn't. One inch made a big difference.

She poured the cereal into a bowl and poured milk on top. She didn't spill a drop.

She looked for lion-shaped pieces. Amy always ate the lions first. She had four trapped in her spoon when the phone rang.

"I'll get it." Amy got up and ran over to the phone.

"Tell whoever it is I can't talk now," her mother said without looking up from her papers at the kitchen table.

It was Mrs. Muldoon.

"I'd like to speak to your mother," she said. Her voice sounded faint and far away.

"Mom's busy," Amy said politely. "She can't come to the phone right now." Amy tried to sound the way her mother sounded.

Mrs. Muldoon groaned.

"Can I take a message?"

Mrs. Muldoon groaned again. "I'm not feeling up to snuff," she said. "My stomach's acting up something awful."

"It is!" Amy said. She smiled at the thought of Mrs. Muldoon's stomach acting up. The rest of her hardly ever did. Sitting was her favorite sport.

"That's too bad," Amy said.

"What's too bad?" her mother asked, looking up from her papers.

Amy put her hand over the phone and whispered, "Mrs. Muldoon's sick. She says her stomach is acting up."

"She can still come, can't she?" Her mother had a worried look on her face.

"You can still come, can't you?" Amy repeated into the phone.

There was a louder groan.

Amy shrugged. Her mother pushed her chair back and took three giant steps to the phone.

"Now, what's this about your stomach?" she asked.

Amy finished her cereal. She wasn't looking for lions now. She was listening.

She couldn't hear what Mrs. Muldoon was saying. But her mother was saying, "I see. I see." She was tapping her foot, which meant she was mad. Amy was glad she wasn't mad at her.

"But today is the day of my sales meeting," her mother said. "I *have* to be there. Why didn't you call earlier?"

Amy tiptoed to the sink with her empty bowl.

She sloshed it in soapy water. Then she picked up a dish towel to dry it. Her mother slammed down the phone and sighed. Her sigh was almost as big as one of Amy's.

"Mrs. Muldoon can't come," her mother said. She stirred her coffee so hard it spilled all over. "She says she's sick. She says she didn't

call earlier because she thought she'd get better."

"I don't know what to do." Her mother put her head in her hands. "I just don't know."

"I don't either," her father said, shaking his head. "I have to be at the plant. The regional manager is coming and it's my job to show him around."

Amy took a deep breath. "I know what to do," she said very slowly. "I can baby-sit myself. I can stay home alone. I won't make a mess, or touch the stove, or let anyone in, or be scared. Or anything. I'll show you I'm big enough. Please."

THREE

AMY'S mother looked at her father. Her father looked back at her mother.

Neither spoke. Amy's eyes darted from the one to the other.

"You'll see," Amy said. "Everything will be okay."

"There must be someone else," Amy's father fretted.

"That's the problem with living in such a small building," Amy's mother said, shaking her head. "The Chans have a new baby and everyone else works except grouchy Mr. Sadler."

"Then can I?" Amy leaned closer and asked.

"The building is pretty secure," her father said.

"And it won't be for long," her mother said.

"Then can I?" Amy repeated.

They both looked at each other again. Then they both sighed and said, "Okay. I guess."

"Whoopee!" Amy threw the dish towel into the air as her mother added, "*If* Mrs. Sanchos can bring you home."

Why was there always an "if"? Amy held her breath while her mother called Mrs. Sanchos. She had twin boys, a year older than Amy, at the same school.

Mrs. Sanchos said it was fine, and Amy was so happy she did the rest of the dishes too.

Now everyone was busy. Amy's father cut carrot sticks and made Amy an after-school sandwich. Her mother wrote "Refrigerator Rules and Important Phone Numbers" on a piece of her paper.

"I won't be near a phone," she said as she wrote. "But you can always call in an emergency. Tell whoever answers it's important, and to get me."

"I'll call Amy," her father said.

"I'll be here," Amy said with a smile.

Her mother went over the refrigerator rules

and phone numbers with Amy. Amy put the paper on the refrigerator with a flower magnet.

REFRIGERATOR RULES

1. Don't let ANYONE in for ANY reason.
2. Don't tell anyone you're at home alone. Say "Mom/Daddy can't come right now. May I take a message?"
3. No using the stove or matches.
4. No climbing, no messes.
5. Do your homework.
6. Have fun!!!!

"The most important thing," her mother said, "is to keep the door locked tight. Don't open the door, no matter what."

"I won't," Amy said, crossing her heart.

And then her mother put the apartment key and the extra front-door key on a silver chain. She put the chain around Amy's neck.

Amy liked the feel of the cold keys against her skin. Wearing keys made her feel grown-up and important.

She liked the sound of the click when she turned the apartment key the right way. She

practiced opening and closing the front door till it was time to go.

Amy and her parents walked together to her mother's bus stop. Amy hugged her mother and said, "Thanks for letting me."

"Just remember everything I told you," her mother said as she got on the bus.

"I will. I will," Amy said.

Her father walked her the rest of the way to school. "Love you a bundle and a bunch," he said as he gave her an extralong squeeze at the corner.

"Me too," Amy said as she waved to Ellen, her best friend, over her father's shoulder.

Amy wriggled away and ran to catch up with Ellen. As she did, she called out, "Guess what I get to do?"

FOUR

"YOU'RE lucky," Ellen twisted her hair and said. "I never get to do anything."

"It's no big deal," Chris, another friend, said. "I stay home alone lots. I like having time to myself before everybody else gets home and I get dumped on."

"I've never done it," Amy said as they walked down the hall. "It is a big deal for me."

All day during class, Amy fingered her keys and looked forward to the afternoon. She felt excited and wished the day would go faster. Instead, the afternoon dragged.

But finally it was over. Amy stuffed her books into her book bag and raced out to meet

the Sanchos twins in front of the school.

The twins, Andy and Pedro, looked almost alike. They both had dark, curly hair and big brown eyes. Some people had trouble telling them apart. Amy didn't. Pedro was shorter and had a scar on his forehead from falling off his bike.

Pedro and Andy acted alike too. They were always kidding and clowning around. Today they were playing catch with their schoolbooks when Amy came up and said, "Guess what I get to do?"

"What?" Pedro asked as *The History of the World* crashed to the sidewalk.

"I get to stay home alone," Amy said, dancing around. "Just think. No more Mrs. Muldoon. No more homework before TV. No more dumb game shows. No more yucky tofu." At the thought of tofu, she made a face.

"I never get to do anything." Pedro stuck his lower lip out in a pretend sulk.

"Poor Pedro." Andy gave him a playful poke as their mother came around the corner, shouting, "Boys!"

She rolled her eyes at Amy as she hugged

the twins and said, "Believe me, double trouble."

Pedro and Andy squirmed but smiled.

At the light, Pedro asked, "Why can't we stay home alone? Amy's a whole year younger and she gets to."

"Because you're always fighting," Mrs. Sanchos said as Andy bumped his brother in the behind. "I wouldn't leave you two little monkeys home alone for two minutes."

Amy smiled at getting to do something the twins didn't.

When they got to her building, Amy said, "Thanks," and put the front-door key in the keyhole. Mrs. Sanchos shook her head and edged in the front door first. "Let me go in, to make sure everything is okay."

The twins followed as their mother walked around the lobby, looking in the corners and under the stairs.

"Come," Mrs. Sanchos said. "Everything is okay here. Now we go up." She held the elevator door open and said to Amy, "Never get in an empty elevator with a stranger."

Pedro gave Andy a big shove and giggled,

"That means Andy has to get out. Because he's stranger than anyone."

Pedro laughed, but he was the only one who did.

Amy sighed. She couldn't wait for them to go, so she could do what she wanted.

On the third floor, Amy got out quickly and said, "Thanks again."

But Mrs. Sanchos got out just as quickly and said with a determined look, "I want to make sure everything is okay."

Now Amy was annoyed. Her fingers felt fumbly as she turned the key.

Nothing happened.

Mrs. Sanchos was watching.

Amy turned the key the other way.

Whew! It worked. There was a click and the door opened.

Amy rolled her eyes as Mrs. Sanchos again went ahead and walked around the living room. Mrs. Sanchos then headed for her room, saying, "You wait here. I'll check."

Pedro turned on the living-room TV and plopped down on the sofa.

Andy plopped down on Pedro.

Amy tapped her foot and glared down the long hall. Why did Mrs. Sanchos have to be so fussy? She was even looking behind the shower curtain. Amy could tell. She heard the familiar swish.

"Wow!" both twins said at the same time.

"Wow what?" Amy turned and asked.

"The news lady was talking about a guy called the Chicken Snitcher," Pedro said. "He dresses up in a chicken suit and robs apartments. He leaves claw scratches over everything but no fingerprints."

"Want to see what you missed?" Andy flapped around the room like a chicken waving its claws. As he did, he clucked.

"That's enough," Mrs. Sanchos said as she came back.

"More than enough," Amy said to herself as she held the door open.

"Everything is fine," Mrs. Sanchos said. "Just keep the door closed."

"I will," Amy said.

Mrs. Sanchos gave Amy's arm a little squeeze and added, "And call if you get scared."

"I won't," Amy said. "I mean, thanks but I won't get scared."

"And don't let the Chicken Snitcher get you," Andy clucked one last time.

Amy closed the door behind them with a "Whew."

She turned the bolt, heard the click, Mrs. Sanchos mutter, "Good."

After she heard the creaky elevator door open and close, Amy tossed her school bag into the air and yelled, "Whoopee!"

FIVE

SOME of Amy's schoolbooks spilled out, but she left them where they lay. Without anybody there, it didn't matter.

Amy sat on the soft chair where Mrs. Muldoon always sat. She turned on the TV. At last, she could watch what she wanted. And what she wanted was something exciting. Like "Cartoon Hour" or "Monsterama," which Mrs. Muldoon never let her watch.

Amy played with the buttons on the remote control. She liked making cars, people, and the news disappear at the push of a button.

The only trouble was there weren't any monster shows or cartoons. There was only dumb stuff, including the game show Mrs. Muldoon always watched.

Amy ended up watching "Divorce Court." It was kind of interesting. But not very. There was a lot of boring talk about who got to keep the car and the cat.

Amy switched to "Exercise with Alice." The music was good but the exercises were hard. So she turned the TV off and went into her room to play with Hermie, her hamster.

Hermie was curled up in a ball, sound asleep.

"See you later," Amy said, and went into her parents' room. Her mother didn't like Amy playing with her things. But her mother would never know if Amy put on just a little of her makeup. Amy couldn't wait till she was old enough to wear makeup. She put dark blue on one eye, and purple on the other.

Amy looked at herself in the mirror and liked what she saw. There was plenty of time to wash it off before her mother got home.

Next Amy felt like playing a game. But what game? She walked back to her room and went through all the boxes on her shelf.

Her favorite was under a lot of other stuff. It

was called Jailbirds. She and Ellen played it a lot when Ellen came over.

The pieces were plastic birds. The point was to get the birds out of jail. The first person to get a bird to Freedom Square was the winner.

It was an exciting game. Different things happened when you landed on different squares. Some squares meant you had to start all over again. Others got you out on bail or for good behavior.

Amy played against herself. She played both the red bird and the blue bird. She cheered herself. Then she tried to beat herself. But playing alone wasn't nearly as exciting as playing with Ellen. She missed not knowing what cards were in the other hand. She missed the way Ellen twisted her hair every time she picked up a card. And the way she squealed when she had to go back.

Amy played one game. Then she put Jailbirds away and went back to the kitchen.

She looked at the clock. It was less than an hour that she'd been at home alone. But somehow it seemed longer. She opened the refrigerator and looked for something to eat—

something more exciting than a sandwich.

Aha! She found a slice of cold pizza under the lettuce, and put baloney and cheese spread on it. As she munched, she imagined Mrs. Muldoon saying, "Mercy, child, you can't eat that."

She could. And did. And it was good. It was even better with ketchup. Amy made the carrot sticks her father had cut better too, by dipping them into different things. She tried peanut butter and mayonnaise and grape jelly. The peanut butter was the best.

When she'd finished, she put everything away. Putting things away wasn't fun. But she wanted her parents to say, "Just look how neat everything is. You can stay home alone any day."

SIX

NOW what to do? Amy went back into her room to look for something.

She still felt like playing with Hermie. But Hermie was still asleep.

"Why do you have to be such a sleepyhead?" Amy asked. Even that didn't wake Hermie up.

She saw her basketball under the bed and rolled it out. She bounced it on the floor to see if she could get to twenty bounces without stopping.

At fifteen, she heard three sharp taps.

Amy kicked the ball back under the bed.

Cranky Mr. Sadler lived in the apartment below. He hated noise. He tapped his cane on the ceiling when anyone said boo.

Amy opened her window and made a face at Mr. Sadler through the window bars. She hoped he could feel it.

Now what to do?

Amy pulled out her crayons and drew a picture of Hermie sleeping.

Only it didn't look like Hermie. It looked more like a large, furry jelly bean. Amy didn't know how to draw paws. The harder she tried, the worse they looked.

Mrs. Muldoon was good at drawing. She showed Amy how to draw things. Amy gave up and went back into the living room and turned the TV on again.

There still weren't any good shows on. But it was nice to hear the sound of voices. She left the TV on and hooked her math workbook with her left foot.

Amy decided she might as well get it over with. It was like eating lima beans before dessert. Dessert was reading. Amy liked reading stories.

What she didn't like was not having anyone to talk to. She didn't like not having anyone to

tell, "This is funny," or ask, "What does this word mean?"

Even with the TV on, the apartment seemed quiet, too quiet. It was so quiet it was almost spooky.

SEVEN

TO drown out the quiet, Amy kept the TV on.

To drown out the spooky feeling, she decided to call Ellen. It was the one number she always remembered. She wanted to say, "Guess what I just played?" She also wanted to ask about the math problems. But mainly she just wanted to chat.

Ellen wasn't home. And nobody else was home to tell Amy where Ellen was. Maybe Ellen and Chris were playing together. Amy felt left out thinking about it. She thought of calling Chris to find out. But she didn't remember the number. She wished more of her friends' numbers were on the refrigerator list.

Then the phone rang.

"Hello," Amy said excitedly. Maybe it was Ellen, or Chris, or her father.

"Hello, Amy," a too familiar voice said. Amy's face fell. It was Mrs. Sanchos.

"I just called to see how you are."

"Fine," Amy said.

"And how you are doing?"

"Fine."

"I have to go out soon, and I just wanted to make sure."

"I'm sure I'm fine."

Amy was annoyed. It was as if Mrs. Sanchos expected something to be wrong.

"Is Andy there?" Amy asked to change the subject.

"No."

"Pedro?"

"They're both with their father," Mrs. Sanchos said.

Amy was oddly disappointed. Pedro and Andy weren't her favorite friends. But right now Amy felt like asking, "Know a good joke?" She felt like hearing a joke, even a bad one.

Amy hung up and took another look at the

refrigerator list. She didn't call Gram because Gram lived too far away.

She didn't call Mrs. Muldoon because she didn't know what to say. She didn't dare say, "Sorry you're not here," when she wasn't sorry. The weird thing was that, in a way, Amy did miss Mrs. Muldoon.

Weirdest of all, she missed her parents, a lot. She also knew they didn't like being interrupted.

Besides, there wasn't an emergency.

It was just that Amy was lonely—something she hadn't expected to be.

EIGHT

AMY didn't know what she felt like doing.

Cookies! she said to herself. I'll make no-bake cookies like the ones we made in school. That way I won't have to touch the stove, or anything.

She imagined the pleased looks on her parents' faces when she said, "Surprise and welcome home!"

She imagined her mother taking a tiny bite and saying, "Delicious." She imagined her father eating one whole and saying, "Don't tell Gram, but they're even better than hers. I don't know how you did it."

She imagined Mrs. Muldoon trying one and saying, "Just what I needed to feel better."

She imagined her teacher telling the whole class how much better they were "than the ones we did."

She even imagined a cookie company calling and saying, "We have to have that recipe."

She could see her picture on the stacked boxes of Amy's Peanut Butter Cookie Balls at the Mini Mart.

She saw herself on a TV talk show chatting about how she got the idea one afternoon at home alone.

Then Amy set to work. She was happy and humming as she took the ingredients out.

Being busy helped get rid of the spooky, lonely feeling.

Amy put everything on the kitchen counter. She didn't remember the recipe from school, so she made one up using some of the same things, like peanut butter. Peanut butter made anything better. She liked crunchy best. Amy mixed it with margarine and plenty of graham cracker crumbs.

She mixed and smooshed it around until it felt, and tasted, right. She tried using a fork. But her fingers worked better and were easier to lick.

Again she smooshed and tasted. Yum! Then she rolled everything into one big ball and divided the big ball into three smaller balls.

She smooshed raisins in one, chocolate bits in another, and shredded coconut in the other. Then she made the three cookie balls into small, bite-size balls, put sugar in a bag, and shook some of the balls in it. She stuck pieces of candy corn in the others.

Amy put the finished cookie balls on her mother's best plate, the one they used on holidays, and put the plate in the refrigerator.

Thirsty from all that tasting, she made a quick grab for the orange juice.

Oops, her hand slipped. The carton tipped over. Orange juice fell like a waterfall. Soon there was a big, sticky orange puddle on the floor. Amy sighed, grabbed a roll of paper towels, and started mopping up.

Then the phone rang.

Amy wiped one hand against her dress and picked up the wall phone.

"How's everything going?" her father asked in a cheerful voice.

"Okay," Amy said. The wad of soaked tow-

els in her other hand was dripping down her dress. Little orange rivers were making new little orange puddles on the floor.

"Just okay?" he asked. "You're sure?"

"I'm sure." Amy said. She was sure she didn't want to tell her father about the spilled orange juice.

"So, what are you up to?" her father asked.

"Oh. Nothing," Amy said. She didn't want to tell about the cookies either. That would spoil her surprise.

"Nothing?"

"I did most of my math. But I couldn't do it all. And I read some."

"You're not lonely, are you?"

"I'm fine," Amy said, anxious to get back to wiping up.

"I miss you," her father said. "I'll be home in about two hours."

"Hmmm," Amy said as she tried to stop a new orange juice river from running down her leg.

Then she said, "Bye, Daddy."

"You're not trying to get rid of me, are you?" her father said in his teasing voice.

"Don't be silly," Amy said.

Then she hung up and went back to cleaning.

She was wiping furiously when she heard something. It was a high, sharp sound.

Amy stopped and listened.

The sound stopped too.

Then it started again. It went scritch-scratch, scritch-scratch.

Amy sucked in her breath. What could it be? It was a sound she had never heard before. And it was coming from her room.

Or was it?

Amy squeezed the sticky towels. Aha! She thought of the TV cable that flopped against her building in the wind.

She looked out the kitchen window. There wasn't any wind. The branches on the little tree near the next building were still. And the cable was tied.

As she looked, the sound stopped again. Then it started again. Scritch-scratch, scritch-scratch. The high, whiny noise sounded like somebody sawing something. Amy had a scary thought. What if somebody was sawing at the window bars in her room?

Why had she opened her bedroom window?

NINE

AMY took a deep breath.

The sound stopped.

But not for long.

She sat, hands folded, and tried to calm herself. The next building was a wide space away. Nothing could come in her window.

Or could it?

Amy then tried to think of a sensible reason for the sound.

Her mother believed in reasons. Once, when she was little, Amy had wailed, "There are ghosts in my room."

Her mother had held her and told her, "There is a sensible reason for most things that seem scary. Curtains blowing in the wind may look like ghosts. But they are still just curtains."

Amy thought back to another time when she was in bed and heard a crash. "It's the closet monster," she had screamed. The closet monster was big and blobby. He had suction cups instead of hands. And Amy had bad dreams about him.

Her father had taken her into the hall. He had opened the hall closet door and said, "See, a shelf fell. There's no closet monster. Just a closet mess. Pumpkin, your imagination has a way of running away with itself."

Now the sound stopped again. Amy got up and tiptoed down the long hall. She decided to look for a sensible reason.

She stopped in front of the hall closet. She counted to ten and yanked the door open. The floor was messy, but there was nothing to explain the scritch-scratch.

Amy needed something new to take her mind off that noise, so she started putting the jumble of boots and shoes in pairs. A neat closet would be a nice surprise for her parents too.

Amy was groping for her other red boot

when the sound started again. Only louder.

Now Amy was sure it was coming from her room. Something *was* there.

A feeling of scare shot from Amy's stomach to her throat. She had to get out of there.

Amy backed out of the closet and edged along the wall to the kitchen. The hall was long. Maybe *it* hadn't heard her.

Amy closed the kitchen door and leaned against it. Her breath came in quick gasps. Her insides felt hollow. She twisted her hair and debated what to do. Ellen twisted her hair a lot. Amy only did it when she was really upset.

Part of her wanted to run out of the apartment. But where would she go? Besides, she had promised not to open the door. Another part wanted to march right into her room and say, "Okay, who are you? And what do you want?"

But she was too scared.

The biggest part wanted to hide. Maybe *it* would take what it wanted and go away.

Amy scrunched herself under the kitchen table. The plastic tablecloth helped hide her. The

floor was still sticky from the juice, but that didn't matter now.

Amy's thoughts raced wildly. She pictured all the scary things *it* might be.

What if *it* was a robber breaking in?

Or a kidnapper?

What if the bogeyman really was real? And *it* was one?

What if *it* was a monster rat sharpening its teeth?

Pedro once told her, "Rats have teeth that keep on growing. That's why a rat gnaws things—to keep its teeth from falling out of its face."

Another wild thought. What if there was an alien spaceship on the roof above her? What if one-eyed *its* planned to kidnap her? Maybe the weird scritch-scratch was an alien.

Then Amy had the scariest thought of all. What if *it* was the Chicken Snitcher? The Chicken Snitcher *was* real. He'd been on the news. And the scritch-scratch really sounded like chicken claws ripping up the place.

Amy shuddered. And what would it do if it found her?

By now, one foot was asleep. Amy's throat was dry and she had to go to the bathroom.

More than anything, she missed her parents, so badly it was like a toothache. She ached to be held and told, "There, there. Everything's okay. It was just a bad dream. It isn't real."

But the scritch-sound *was* real, and so was her fear.

Amy stared at the kitchen clock. Each minute tick seemed to take forever. Two hours, her father had said.

Then the phone rang. Amy jumped up but quickly scrunched back down. Her father had already called and her mother had said she wouldn't be able to.

Amy covered her ears to drown out the sound. She wondered why she ever wanted to stay home alone. Then the ringing stopped. And so did the scritch-scratch sound. The silence was even scarier. Amy couldn't help it. She cried.

She cried a long time.

She was almost cried out when she heard elevator noises. The door on her floor opened and closed. Then she heard footsteps.

She felt a small ping of hope. Maybe her parents were coming home.

She looked at the clock. No, it was too soon. It had to be someone else.

But who?

Then Amy heard the apartment key click. Someone or something was coming in.

Scare turned to terror, blotting out everything. Now she was trapped. That was the worst.

TEN

AMY barely heard the frantic voices calling, "Amy! Amy!"

"In here," Amy said weakly.

Her mother gasped at the sight of Amy under the kitchen table with big smudges of makeup under her eyes.

"What happened?" her father asked. He sounded angry.

Amy started crying again. She pointed down the hall.

Her mother hugged her. Her father kept asking "Amy, what happened? And why didn't you pick up the phone when I called?"

"I did," Amy said in a snuffly voice.

"Not the second time," her father said. "I called back because you sounded funny. I was worried sick. What's wrong?"

"I spilled the orange juice," Amy said between sobs. "I wanted to wipe it up so you wouldn't be mad. And I used some of Mom's eye makeup."

"All this over a little eye shadow and spilled juice?" Her father slapped his hand hard against the table. "Amy, I still want to know why you didn't pick up the phone the second time I called."

"I was scared."

"Of what?"

"Of *it*."

"What it?"

"I don't know what kind of it," Amy said, and shrugged. "The *it* that was going to grab me if it heard me. Which was why I couldn't get up and get the phone. I was hiding from *it*."

"Where is *it* now?" he asked.

Amy pointed down the hall again. "Listen. Just listen. It goes scritch-scratch. You'll hear it."

Amy's parents cupped their ears and listened.

After a minute, her father shook his head, "I don't hear a thing."

"I don't either," her mother said, frowning.

"Sometimes *it* lies still and waits," Amy said

Her mother gave her father a funny look.

Amy bit her lip. Her parents were home. But everything was worse.

Not being believed was worse than being scared.

"You think I'm lying, don't you?" Amy cried harder than ever.

"What I think," her father said, "is that you have a pretty vivid imagination." He put his arm around her as he said it. "Sometimes things seem scary when you're alone. I also think we should have known better than to—"

He was interrupted by scritch-scratch, scritch-scratch.

Amy sighed with relief. She didn't think she'd ever wanted to hear that sound again. Now she was glad.

"Stay here, you two." Her father's eyes flashed. He grabbed the big frying pan and charged down the hall.

Amy could still hear the scritch-scratch. Then there was a loud, "Aha!" And then a laugh, "Well, I'll be . . ."

"What is it?" Amy's mother held Amy close and asked.

"Come see for yourself," Amy's father called from Amy's doorway.

"There it is. There's your monster, Amy." He grinned as he pointed his finger at something. And as the awful scritch-scratch kept on.

The something was Hermie, going around and around on his exercise wheel. Only the wheel wasn't going around right. It was going lopsided. At each turn, the sides grated against the cage bars. The grating made the scritch-scratch sound. The sound stopped as Hermie stopped to look at everybody looking at him. When he got back on, the scritch-scratch started again.

"What an awful screechy sound," Amy's mother said, putting her hands over her ears. "But thank goodness it was nothing."

"It wasn't nothing to me!" Amy flung herself on her bed and buried her face in her panda pillow.

"Now you'll think I'm still a baby," she said without looking up. "And never let me do anything again. Ever."

ELEVEN

"I DON'T think you're a baby," Amy's father said gently.

He sat on the edge of her bed and rubbed Amy's back. "Being scared isn't babyish. Believe me, I'm no baby, and I was plenty scared when I couldn't reach you."

"You were?"

"Me too." Amy's mother sat next to her father. "I was scared silly."

"You were?" Amy raised her head a little.

"Know what?" her mother said.

"What?"

"I think you were very brave to be scared and not panic."

"I did, sort of," Amy admitted.

"But you didn't leave the apartment or let anyone in, or do anything foolish," her father said.

"I didn't feel brave either," Amy said into her pillow.

"But you were!" her father said.

"And I am very proud of you," her mother added softly.

"You are?" Amy raised her head up all the way.

"We both are," her father said. "I'm the one who feels silly." He waved the frying pan at Hermie. It was like a go signal. Hermie started going around faster. The scritch-scratch got louder.

"Then can I stay home alone again?" Amy asked above the scritch-scratch.

"Do you want to?" her mother asked.

"Maybe not tomorrow," Amy said. "And not all the time. But sometime. Only next time I want more of my friends' numbers to call. And I want more games and things to do by myself. And maybe Chris and I could start an At Home Alone Club for doing homework and just talking."

"What a good idea." Her mother gave Amy a pat on the back. "You are full of good ideas."

"Only next time, call," Amy's father said. "It doesn't have to be an emergency."

"But I thought you didn't want to be bothered."

"Bothered?" her father repeated. "You are not a bother. Ever. You are what matters most, more than any meeting or any job. More than anything. Always remember that.

"And now I'd better fix the monster cage," he added with a wink.

"And I'd better call Mrs. Muldoon to see if she'll be back tomorrow," her mother said. "That is, if we want her."

"Kind of," Amy said as she picked Hermie up and put him in her pocket, "because I made some—"

Amy's hand flew to her mouth as she remembered her cookie balls.

"What is it?" her parents asked.

"I forgot something important," Amy wailed.

"Forgot what?"

"Your coming-home surprise," Amy said

on the run. "My Amy's Peanut Butter Cookie Balls."

She came back from the kitchen with the plate. "Ta-rah!" She held it out. "I made them all by myself. I even made up the recipe."

Amy's mother took a bite and said, "Delicious."

Her father popped a whole cookie ball into his mouth and said, "Hmmmm, that really hits the spot. How did you do it?"

"I just smooshed everything together," Amy said, pleased that they were pleased.

Her father took another and said, "I think one treat deserves another. Let's go to McDonald's as soon as I fix Hermie's cage."

"Whoopee!" Amy said, giving Hermie a pat.

On the way, Amy walked between her mother and her father. She felt like the jam in a family sandwich. It was a cosy feeling.

When they were almost there, Amy tugged at her father's sleeve and said, "Can I ask you something?"

"Shoot."

"When will I be big enough to go to McDonald's all by myself?"

"Whoa!" Her father stopped walking and looked at Amy.

"When will you stop being in such a hurry to be big?" her mother asked with a smile.

"When I am," Amy said, and smiled back.

AMY'S PEANUT BUTTER COOKIE BALLS

12 oz chunky or smooth **PEANUT BUTTER**
2 sticks **MARGARINE**
1 pound **CONFECTIONERS' SUGAR**
2 cups **GRAHAM CRACKER CRUMBS**
CHOCOLATE CHIPS, RAISINS,
or **SHREDDED COCONUT**
if desired, to taste

Mix by hand, roll into balls.
Dip in confectioners' sugar.
Let harden in the refrigerator.
Enjoy!